Food +

THIS BOOK BELONGS TO

....

For Charlie and Daisy

OXFORD

UNIVERSITY PRESS

Great Clarendon Street, Oxford OX2 6DP

Oxford University Press is a department of the University of Oxford.
It furthers the University's objective of excellence in research,
scholarship, and education by publishing worldwide in

Oxford New York
Auckland Cape Town Dar es Salaam Hong Kong Karachi
Kuala Lumpur Madrid Melbourne Mexico City Nairobi
New Delhi Shanghai Taipei Toronto

With offices in
Argentina Austria Brazil Chile Czech Republic France Greece
Guatemala Hungary Italy Japan Poland Portugal Singapore
South Korea Switzerland Thailand Turkey Ukraine Vietnam

Oxford is a registered trade mark of Oxford University Press
in the UK and in certain other countries

Text and illustrations © Caroline Jayne Church 2006

Database right Oxford University Press (maker)

First published 2006

British Library Cataloguing in Publication Data available

ISBN-13; 978-019-279162-7 (hardback)
ISBN-10: 0-19-279162-1 (hardback)
ISBN-13: 978-019-279163-4 (paperback)
ISBN-10: 0-19-279163-X (paperback)

10 9 8 7 6 5 4 3 2 1

Printed in China

SCRUFF SHEEP

Caroline Jayne Church

OXFORD
UNIVERSITY PRESS

Down on the farm, Scruff Sheep was always late for everything. He was late for feeding time. He was late at night-time.

Whenever it was time for Scruff Sheep to be anywhere . . .

he was usually somewhere else,
in a world of his own.

One spring morning, it was time
for the farmer to shear his flock.

Each sheep was shaved . . .

and clipped . . .

and trimmed.

The flock felt very smart and tidy.
All of them, that is, except one . . .

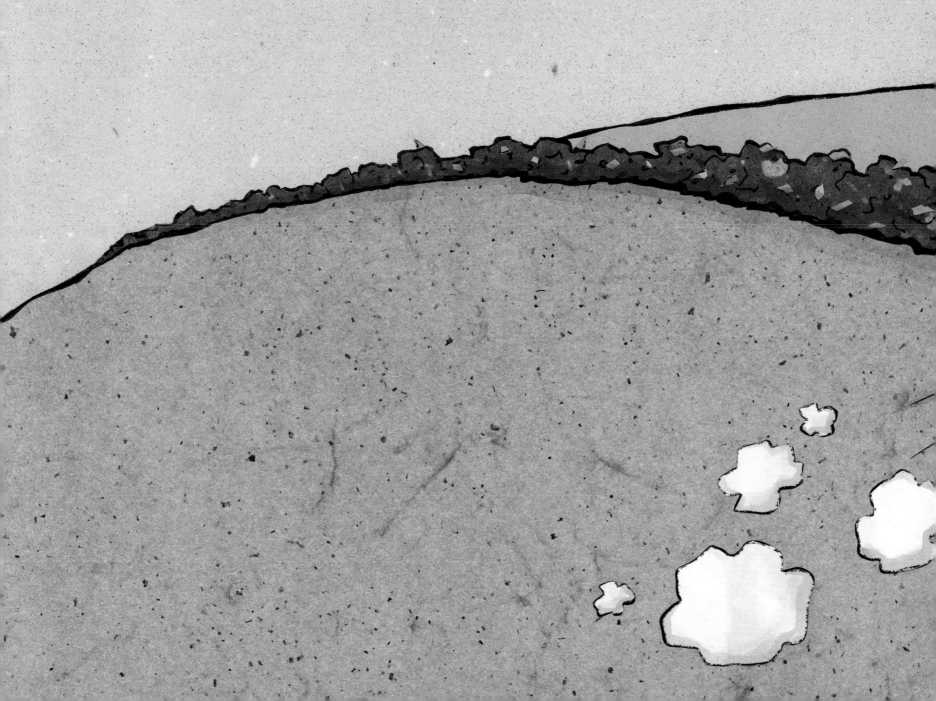

Suddenly, Scruff Sheep
remembered where he should be.

He charged across fields,
jumped over hedges and ditches . . .

but he was too late . . . again.

'You're a shaggy Scruff Sheep,' bleated the others.
'And you're always late for everything.'

Scruff Sheep was upset.

Feeling glum, he wandered off.
He wanted to be alone.

'I'm a late-for-everything, good-for-nothing
Scruff Sheep,' he said to himself.

As he walked past the hen house,
he heard a noise. It was Little Hennie,
crying as if her heart would break.

'Whatever's the matter?' asked Scruff Sheep.
'A nasty tabby cat,' sobbed Little Hennie,
'has frightened the other hens away so now
I'm the only one left to keep all the eggs warm.
But I'm far too small.'

Scruff Sheep knew what to do.
He lay down in the hay and spread
out his long, woolly coat.
Then he told Little Hennie to roll
each egg gently underneath.

Scruff Sheep and Little Hennie snuggled close together. Very soon, they were fast asleep and they didn't wake up until . . . in the morning . . .

they heard a
tap, tap, tap.
A tiny yellow chick hatched
out of every single egg.

Just then the other hens dashed
back into the hen house.
'Thank goodness the nasty
tabby cat has gone,'
they clucked.

'And look, we have a beautiful family of chicks,' squealed Little Hennie.

'It's all thanks to Scruff Sheep.
He came just in time.'
And she gave him a great big hug
and a peck on the cheek.

Scruff Sheep smiled happily.
'I'd better go home,' he said.

Scruff Sheep set off towards the pen.

This time he didn't feel sheepish about being late.

He couldn't wait to tell the others why he was

the hero of the hen house . . .

but they all knew.
For a little bird had already told them!